For Ricky Schober on his first birthday
—S. W.

For Edna and Kenzo
—A. G.

Henry Holt and Company, LLC
*Publishers since 1866*
115 West 18th Street, New York, New York 10011
www.henryholt.com

Henry Holt is a registered trademark of Henry Holt and Company, LLC
Text copyright © 2003 by Sarah Wilson
Illustrations copyright © 2003 by Akemi Gutierrez
All rights reserved.
Distributed in Canada by H. B. Fenn and Company Ltd.

Library of Congress Cataloging-in-Publication Data
Wilson, Sarah. A nap in a lap / Sarah Wilson; illustrated by Akemi Gutierrez.
Summary: Baby animals nap in interesting places, but a tired little girl and
her puppy like to nap in a lap.
[1. Naps (Sleep)—Fiction. 2. Stories in rhyme.] I. Gutierrez, Akemi, ill. II. Title.
PZ8.3.W698 Nap 2003 [E]—dc21 2002012838

ISBN 0-8050-6976-3 / First Edition—2003 / Designed by Donna Mark
Printed in the United States of America on acid-free paper. ∞
10 9 8 7 6 5 4 3 2 1

The artist used gouache on Arches paper to create
the illustrations for this book.

# A Nap in a Lap

Sarah Wilson

*illustrated by* Akemi Gutierrez

*Henry Holt and Company*

*New York*

# It's easy to nap

tucked into a flap

or wrapped in a coil

or sprawled
upside-down

or cuddled in fur

or feathered in brown

or snuzzled
and fuzzled
and kissed on the nose

or cozied in hay

or the tip of a rose . . .

. . . or cradled in snow

or nestled on rocks

or snoozled in sand dunes

TOMATO

CARROT

CABBAGE

or field grass

or socks . . .

. . . or warmed
in the sea

with a tummy
between

or hugged in a tree

and surrounded by green

or snugged in a nest

or a log

or a cap,

but the best nap for ME . . .

. . . is a nap in a lap!